show starts now

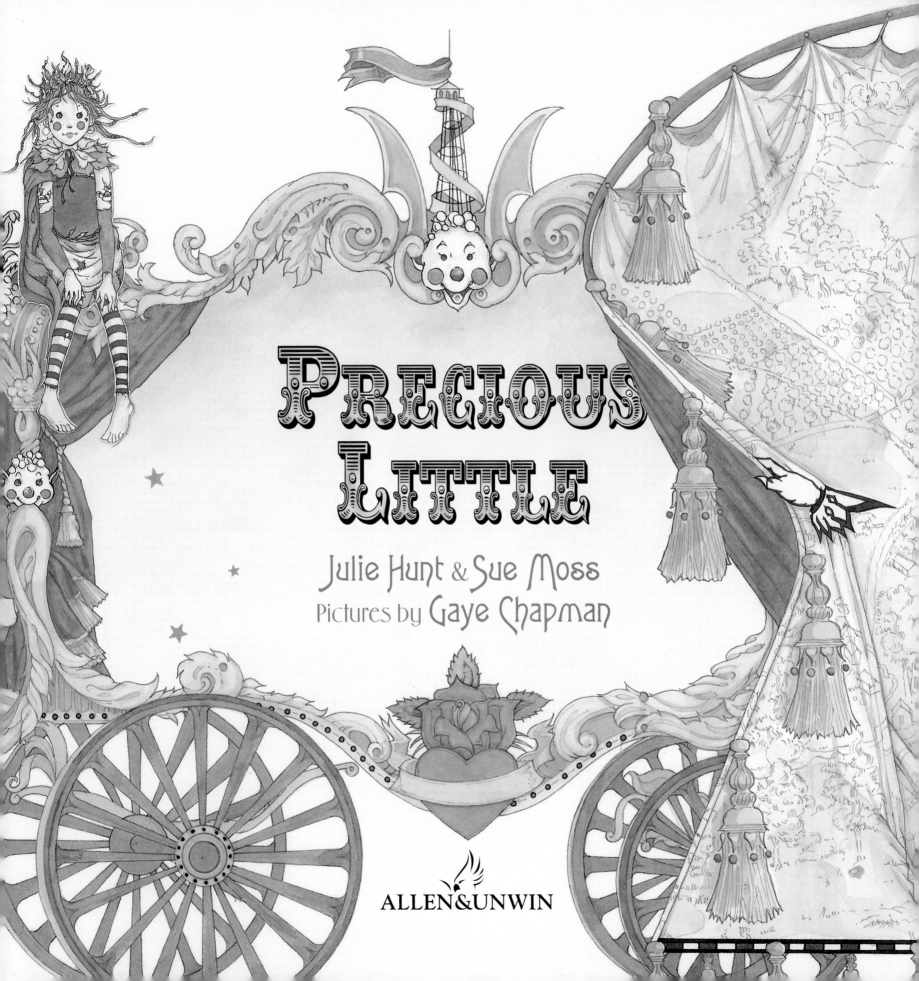

PRECIOUS LITTLE

Julie Hunt & Sue Moss

Pictures by Gaye Chapman

ALLEN&UNWIN

For Nina Prendergast – JH
For Grace Hartshorn & Anna Maria Leitges – SM
For Sue, Debbie, Paulette and Larry Kellner, and Sharlaine Underwood – GC

First published in 2010

Allen & Unwin
83 Alexander St
Crows Nest NSW 2065
Australia
Phone: (61 2) 8425 0100
Fax: (61 2) 9906 2218
Email: info@allenandunwin.com
Web: www.allenandunwin.com

Cataloguing-in-Publication details are available from the National Library of Australia
www.librariesaustralia.nla.gov.au

ISBN 978 174175 147 5

Gaye Chapman used sepia ink line drawings, acrylic ink plus tea-stained paintings,
and collaged metallic papers to create the artwork for this book.

Cover and text design by Gaye Chapman and Sandra Nobes
Set in 20 pt Opti Florentine by Sandra Nobes
This book was printed in April 2010 at Everbest Printing Co Ltd
in 334 Huanshi Road South, Nansha, Guangdong, China.

10 9 8 7 6 5 4 3 2 1

Precious Little wanted to fly

but she was only a circus-hand.
She worked for the Light Fantastics.

Every night she watched them flash through the air. They walked the high wire and did swan dives and double somersaults way up in the big top.

They were brave and strong and they never looked down.

Precious Little practised on the ground. She did wonky cartwheels and fall-over handstands. 'You'll have to do better than that,' they told her.

Precious Little had to sew stars on the Light Fantastics'
costumes. She also cleaned their special shoes and
sifted through the sawdust at the end of each
show looking for lost sequins.

'Join us,' said Knots-R-Us. 'We'll teach you to be a contortionist.' 'Or us,' said Flambé and the Infernos. 'We'll have you eating fire.'

But Precious Little didn't want to eat fire or tie herself in knots.
She drew a line on the ground and walked along it with her eyes shut.

'That's the way,' said her friends, Fat Chance and Tough Luck.
Precious Little sighed. 'Do you think I'll ever fly?' she asked.
'Who knows?' said Tough. 'Keep trying. You're a star to us.'

Fat Chance and Tough Luck ran the lucky dip. They had used up most of their chances years ago but they had high hopes for Precious Little. 'Tell you what,' said Fat. 'Let's give you a go, right now.'

Fat Chance threw a rope across the lucky dip and pulled it tight. Precious Little had never been off the ground before.

The lucky dip was full of sawdust and dreams and it was a long way down. 'I must be brave,' she whispered.

Precious Little stepped out onto the rope. She looked at her feet, then she looked down into the dark swirl of the dip. Her head began to spin.

'She's lost her nerve,' said Tough.

'Keep going!' yelled Fat.

But it was too late.

Precious Little wobbled, then she fell head-first into the dip.

Down, down, down she went.

'Should we go in after her?' cried Fat.

'Give her a chance!' yelled Tough.

precious Little had no idea the dip was so deep or so full.

What prize will you pick from today's lucky dip?

Take the Risk ... or the Scare or the Stunt or the Rip.

You might choose the Joke.

You might take the Chance.

Take the Hope or the Dream or the Song or the Dance.

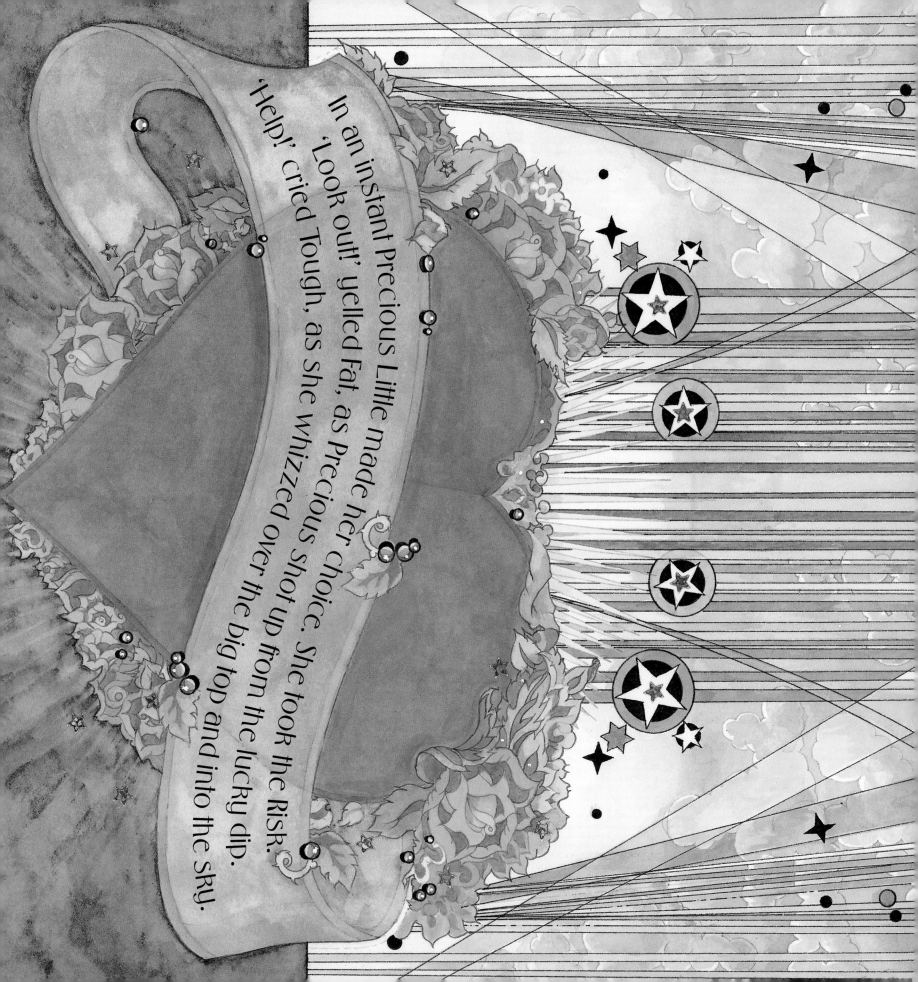

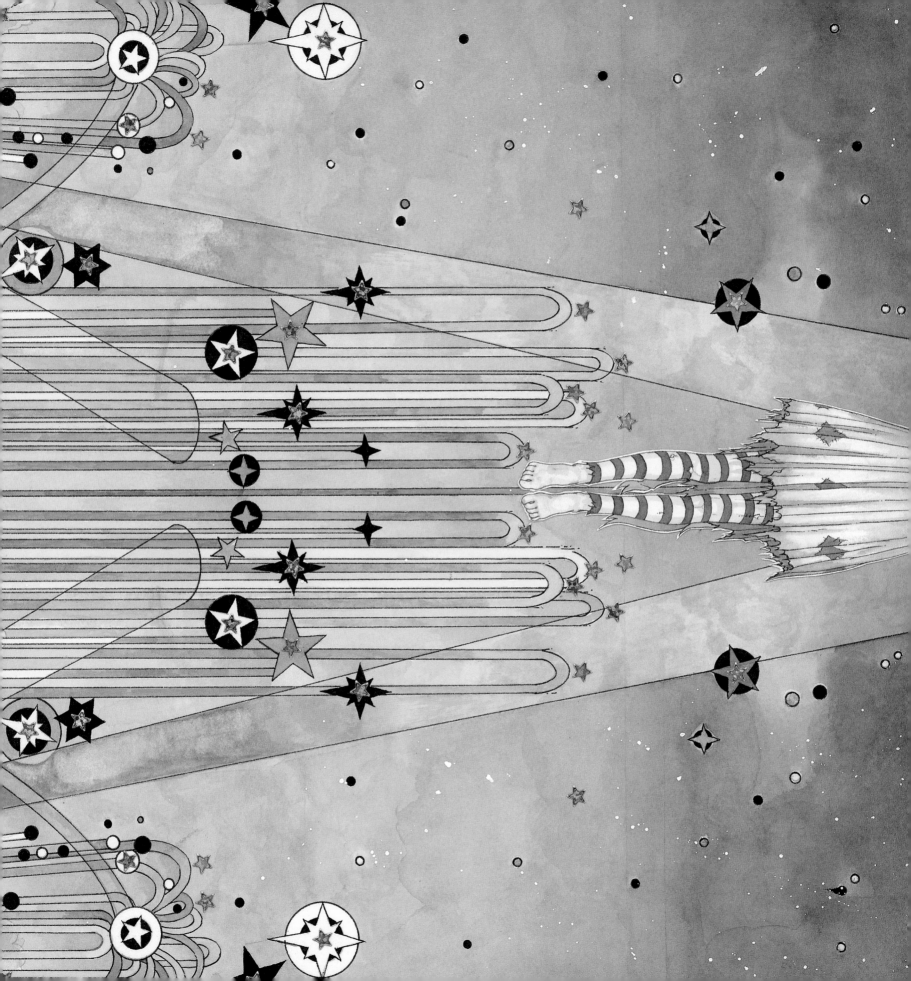

Fat's mouth fell open.
Everyone looked up and waited.
But Precious Little did not come back.
'Now look what you've done!'
cried the Light Fantastics.

'Who's going to sew
the stars on our costumes
and clean our special shoes?'
Fat and Tough hung their heads. 'We've lost her,'
they said. 'We're finished. We're all washed up.'

Time passed. The circus
packed up and moved on.
The paint on Fat and Tough's
caravan faded and snow
covered the spot where the
lucky dip had been.

Up in the sky Precious
Little flew among the stars.

She did swirling cartwheels
and fly-about handstands.
She did galaxy swoops and
over-the-moon backflips.

She was light.
She was fantastic.

She lit up the sky.
She did a triple-twist
star-bursting somersault,
then she circled the earth
with a whiz-around
satellite spin.

She saw the big top and plunged into a spectacular free-falling comet div

Fat Chance and Tough Luck stepped into the centre of the ring.

'Get ready,' cried Fat.

'Here she comes,' yelled Tough.

And they held out their hands and caught her.